Contents

To my parents, who love books

—Alex

CHAPTER 1
Singled Out in Space City

Boo slumped in her seat as the senior class walked into the auditorium and toward the stage. They passed by the fourth grade section, but they might as well have been in one of the Parallel Worlds. There was Lize, singing the school anthem in her high, perfect voice. There was Kira, blonde and confident, the smartest girl in school. There was Marcus, who already had his space-pilot's license. And there was Asano, the school's best slam-ball player until he got thrown off the team.

Asano looked up at Boo's class and smiled as if to say, "Ha ha, you still have eight more years of school."

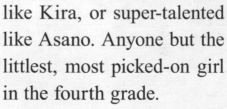

Asano winked at some of the taller girls in Boo's class. The girls giggled and waved.

But Asano hadn't even seen Boo, because she was so small. For the five hundredth time, Boo wished that she would grow. That one morning she'd wake up tall and pretty like Kira, or super-talented like Asano. Anyone but the littlest, most picked-on girl in the fourth grade.

Then an electric silence filled the huge auditorium.

A thousand students leaned forward in their

seats, and a hundred seniors stood straighter on the stage.

At last, the Agents were making their entrance.

The Agents! Boo stretched herself as tall as she could to look. The Agents built this city—Space City, the very center of the Multiverse. From the Aerie, Space City's highest tower, the Agents kept law and order across a thousand parallel worlds.

The Agents! Every kid in Space City grew up on stories of their adventures. The Arachnoverse War . . . The Madrassa Incident . . . Agent Erik's heroic sacrifice . . . Misery's Exile . . .

The Agents! Their job was so dangerous that each autumn they would pick new trainees from the senior class to replace the Agents who had fallen in the course of duty. That's what they were doing now.

The Supreme Agent stepped forward.

"We have three vacancies at the Aerie." Her voice rang out across the auditorium, calm and proud. "As is tradition, each fallen Agent's companion will today select a new master."

"Quoth, do you see a student you would choose as Master, and advise in the ways of being an Agent?" the Supreme Agent said to a bright-eyed raven.

The raven shook his wings, flew up in the air, and looked down on the senior class. Marcus bit his lip nervously. Kira stepped closer to him and took his hand.

Asano rolled his eyes and made a loud kissing sound.

Kira glared at Asano. "Bring it," Asano hissed back.

"Though he is to Erik as day is to night,
My choice could be no other.
So it is with pride and great delight
I select my late Master's brother,"

recited the raven, landing on the shoulder of . . .

. . . Asano! "Well, that figures," said one of the girls sitting near Boo. "I mean, his brother DID save the Multiverse."

Asano reached up, dizzy with wonder, to scratch the feathers of his new friend and partner. "Join us, Agent Asano," said the Supreme Agent, holding out her hand.

Proudly, Asano walked over to where the Agents stood, not forgetting to stick his tongue out at Kira as he walked by. Aghast, Quoth the raven whispered to Kira, "Apologies, Miss; he's new at this."

"That's okay," said Kira to the raven. "Good luck."

Next came a small badger.

"Seeker, do you see a student you would choose as Master, and advise in the ways of being an Agent?"

The badger chewed his paw and glanced at the seniors. His voice was thin and faint.

"I'm just a wee, timorous beastie, an' adventures give me a panic! I need a Master courageous and true. So I pick . . ."

A thousand students held their breath as the shy little badger waddled toward the ninety-nine seniors and reached out a quaking paw to . . .

. . . Kira! Kira swept Seeker up in her arms and smoothed all his fur. Immediately, Seeker stopped shaking.

“Join us, Agent Kira,” said the Agent Leader.

As Kira left the seniors, she winked at Marcus and whispered, “See you soon.”

Now from the Agents strode a big ginger cat, twitching his tail in a rocksteady beat as his eyes swept the auditorium like green searchlights.

“Pumpkin, do you see a student—”

“Yeah, yeah, yeah, Master, advise, Agent,” the cat interrupted. “Lemme have a look-see at what we got.” And with that, he strutted up to the seniors.

Lize flicked her hair and sang a few perfect notes. But Pumpkin just sighed and walked on. An athlete named Will grinned and flexed his perfect muscles. But Pumpkin shook his head and walked on. Then came Marcus, who turned his shoulder to show Pumpkin the badge he’d earned for his perfect score on the space-pilot’s exam . . .

MAYBE THE THIRD ONE'S THE CHARM.
SPACE ACE
SPACE ACE
SPACE CE
OH, BROTHER.
LOOK, I CAN'T DO THIS ANYMORE.

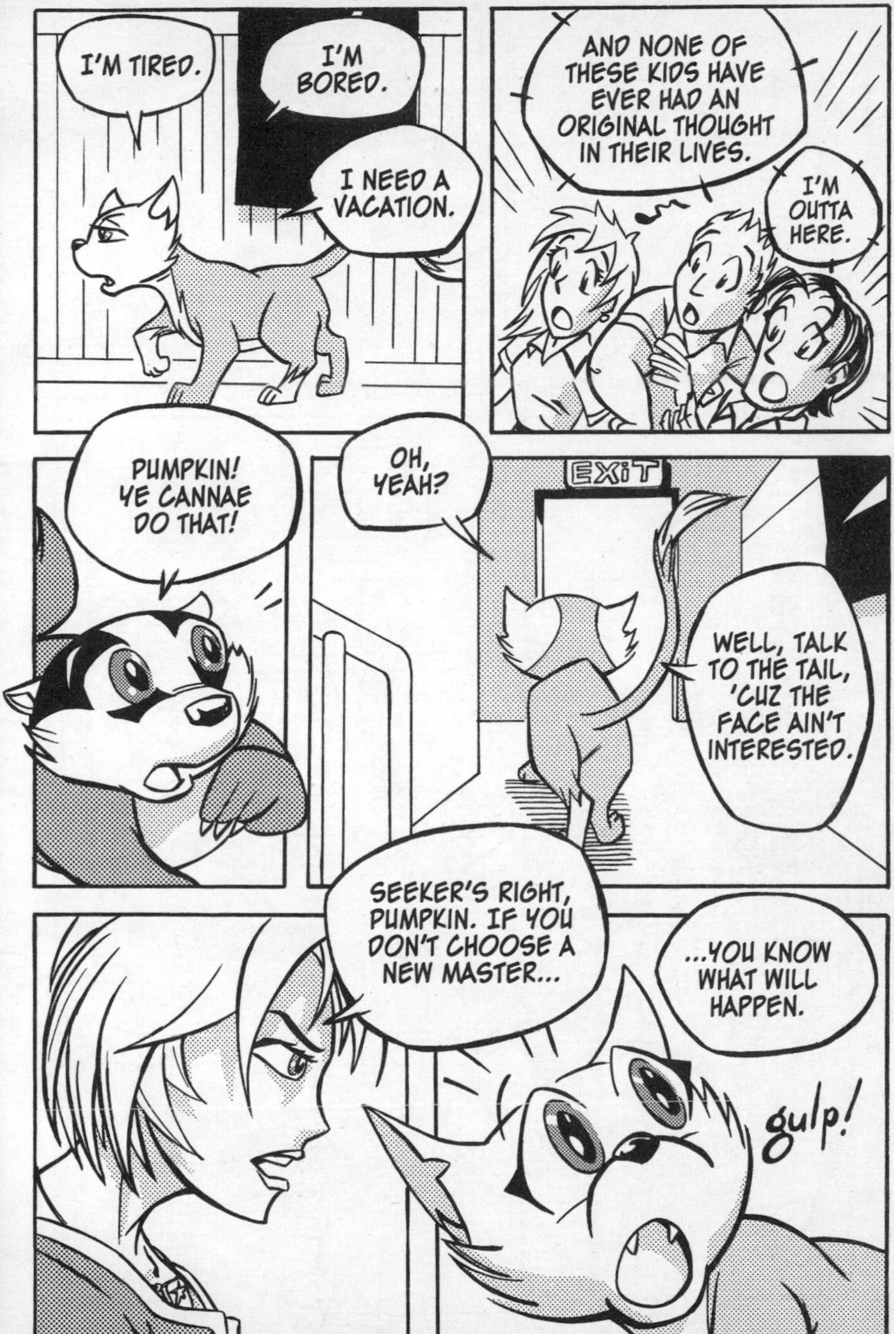
I'M TIRED.
I'M BORED.
I NEED A VACATION.
AND NONE OF THESE KIDS HAVE EVER HAD AN ORIGINAL THOUGHT IN THEIR LIVES.
I'M OUTTA HERE.
PUMPKIN! YE CANNAE DO THAT!
OH, YEAH?
EXIT
WELL, TALK TO THE TAIL, 'CUZ THE FACE AIN'T INTERESTED.
SEEKER'S RIGHT, PUMPKIN. IF YOU DON'T CHOOSE A NEW MASTER...
...YOU KNOW WHAT WILL HAPPEN.
gulp!

ALL RIGHT.
FINE.
WHATEVER.
I CHOOSE...
YOU!

"Hey! That's not fair!" yelled one of the seniors on the stage.

"Yeah, well, for those of you not keeping score, LIFE'S NOT FAIR," Pumpkin roared.

"Pumpkin . . . are you SURE of your choice?" asked the Supreme Agent.

Her second-in-command, Agent Abbot, hurriedly consulted a notebook. "There's no rule against it," he whispered.

The Supreme Agent sighed and extended her hand. "Nothing we can do, then. Very well. Join us, Agent . . . er . . ."

"Boo," squeaked Boo.

". . . Agent *Boo*."

"Mr. Pumpkin . . . um . . . I don't think I'm right for this. I'm not smart or special or anything," Boo whispered urgently to Pumpkin. "Or even very big—"

"I know," said the cat. "And it's gonna drive them bat-crazy when you do just as well as them. Come on, kiddo—time's a-wastin'!"

CONTROVERSY AT TODAY'S
AGENT EVER

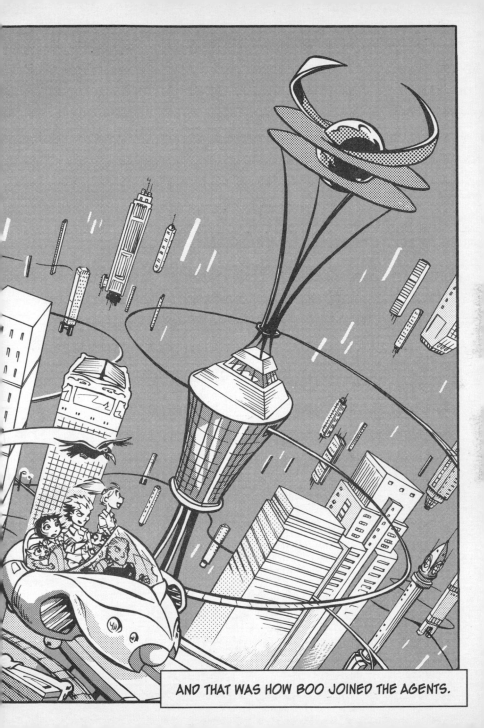

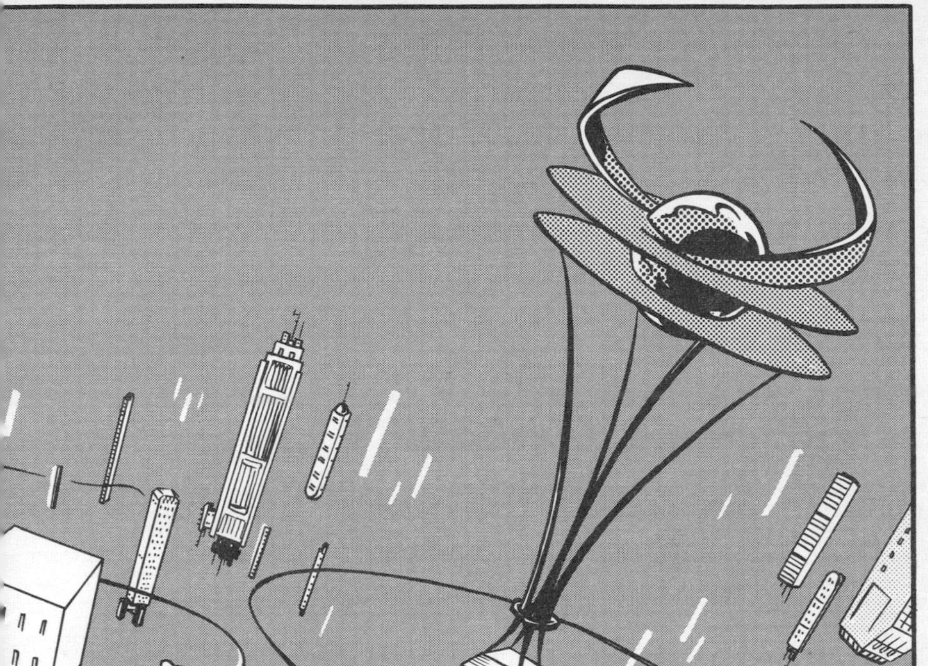
AND THAT WAS HOW BOO JOINED THE AGENTS.

CHAPTER 2
The Agents' Aerie

Agent Abbot, in charge of training, strode down the corridor and consulted his notes. "Agents Kira and Boo, Room 6," he said.

Then the gray-haired Agent looked around and noticed someone was missing.

"Agent Boo? AGENT BOO!"

"Sorry . . . sir . . . !" Boo puffed, out of breath. Boo was so short that when Agent Abbot walked, she had to run. "Sir . . . what's an . . . Artifact? I saw . . . a door . . ."

"Artifacts are not to be touched by trainees!" Agent Abbot barked. "Here's your room; your uniforms and schedules are inside. Your first lesson starts in an hour. Get moving, Agents!"

"Yes, Agent Abbot, sir!" Kira and Boo shouted in chorus.

"Oh—and Kira? Could you keep an eye on Agent Boo? You know . . . make sure she doesn't get into trouble?"

"Yes, sir. I'd be happy to," Kira said proudly.

"Hey! What am I, chopped tuna?" demanded Pumpkin.

"No, Pumpkin. You just have a different definition of 'trouble' than the rest of us," said Agent Abbot as he left.

Asano stuck his bleached-blond head around the door. "Ha ha. Kira got stuck with babysitting duty!"

"Hsssss!" Pumpkin said, baring his teeth and claws at Asano.

Asano ran off, laughing. "Right on. See you in class."

Boo sat down on her new bed and closed her eyes, trying hard not to cry. Kira sat down next to Boo.

"To tell you the truth, I'm a little homesick," she said. "It'll be nice to have a roommate."

"Really?" said Boo.

"Really," said Kira. "Hey, let's try on our uniforms!"

"I wonder what 'Secret History' is," said Boo, looking at the class list.

"Oh, all the stuff we don't tell civilians," said Pumpkin. "How the Parallel Worlds work . . . y'know, the *real* stories behind the legends."

"Omigosh!" Kira said. "Will they tell us about Agent Erik?"

"Aye indeedy," said Seeker. "An' never a braver or truer Agent was there."

"Erik's my hero," Kira blushed. "I even have a poster of him. Do you mind if I put it up?" Boo shook her head.

"I can't believe a creep like Asano is his brother," Kira continued.

Boo stared down at her shiny new Agent boots. It was so cool hanging out with Kira . . . and Kira would know best about Asano, since they were in the same class . . . but Boo couldn't help but think of the time Asano had scared off some bullies that were shoving her around. It wasn't like he really cared or anything . . . but he could have just walked on by.

Boo wanted to mention this to Kira, but she never got the chance. The days were packed, and her head soon felt like it was going to explode from all the lessons.

The parallel worlds . . . the technology the Agents used to travel between them . . . the great battles . . . not to mention the tactics of the Agents' sworn enemies, the Commissars. Boo worked hard and memorized them all.

But then came the Martial Arts lessons. Boo didn't do so well in those.

All this training was for the big Test—the one that would tell if the three new recruits were ready to become full Agents. Those who passed moved on to active duty, policing the Multiverse. Those who didn't . . . got a job in Support. Which sounded important, but really meant getting stuck working in the cafeteria or the library.

Kira was determined to score the highest of the new recruits. Asano was determined to drive Kira crazy. Boo just hoped she got to work in the library, instead of the cafeteria.

CHAPTER 3
The Game of Friends

On the day before the Test, Boo was excused from Martial Arts so she could study. She sat with Pumpkin, memorizing lessons.

"Who's this one again?" Boo asked.

"Kiddo, don't you dare forget her," said Pumpkin, as the hair on the back of his neck bristled. "That's Queen Misery. She's the one who messed up my beautiful ear! Why, if I ever see her again, I'll slice her, I'll dice her, I'll . . . HSSSS!"

Boo drew back in surprise as she looked at the notch in Pumpkin's ear.

"Pumpkin! You're, um . . . spitting."

Pumpkin grudgingly calmed down. "Sorry, kiddo. That woman . . . she just gets me all hot under the flea collar."

"She's scary," said Boo.

"You bet! Queen Misery thinks she and her Commissars should run the Multiverse from Iron City, instead of us running it from Space City. As if anyone would elect *her!"*

"Um . . . but the Agents aren't elected," Boo said.

"Yeah, well . . . that's not the point," said Pumpkin. "We got justice on our side. And have you seen Iron City? What a dump!

Look, I'm a cat—I love to root around in garbage—but even *I* draw the line at *that* place. Yech!"

Suddenly, Kira stomped in and threw her bag on the bed. "Why is Asano SUCH a JERK?!" she screamed.

Seeker peeked around the door, whiskers quivering. "And why can't you keep up with me, Seeker?!" Kira demanded.

The badger slunk into the room.

"Bad day, Seekz?" said Pumpkin.

"Ye dinnae know the half," said Seeker, scuttling under the bed to hide.

"What happened, Kira?" asked Boo.

"OOOH! He makes me so mad!" Kira fumed. "Asano totally messed up this project we were working on. He didn't even read my plan—just made up some stupid stuff from old slam-ball tactics!"

Kira put her hands on her hips and stared at her poster of Erik.

"Why can't Asano just act like his brother? Erik would have read the plan! He wouldn't have just improvised!"

"So . . . did the project fail?" Boo asked.

Kira's lower lip trembled. "No. It worked really well."

Tears welled up in Kira's eyes, but Seeker came out from under the bed and lay a comforting paw on her leg. Kira hugged him. "I'm sorry, Seeker."

"Nae worries, Miss Kira," Seeker said comfortingly. "I know ye dinnae mean it."

"See you later, Boo," Kira sighed. "I'm going to the library to study."

"Okay, see you," said Boo, who had studying of her own to do. But she only got in a few more minutes of work before a shadow fell across the door.

"Yo, Boo," said Asano. "Can I come in for a sec?"

"Sure, Asano," Boo said.

"What is this, Grand Central Station?" grumbled Pumpkin.

"Thanks," Asano said. "I wanted to . . ."

But then his eyes filled with rage as they fell on the poster over Kira's bed.

"No way, man. No. Way."

Asano marched over to the poster, white with anger.

Quoth fluttered his wings in protest. "Master, remember what we discussed! The rules say not to touch others'—!"

But Asano didn't even slow down. He reached up and—RRRRIP!—tore down Kira's poster of Erik.

Boo gasped, but Pumpkin didn't miss a beat. "Oooh, Asano! I'm gonna go make popcorn, so when Kira comes back and kicks your butt, we'll have ringside seats *and* snack food!"

Asano just ignored Pumpkin, tearing the poster into smaller and smaller pieces.

“I’m not my brother, okay?! I know he was all perfect and stuff, but I’m not good at rules and orders like he was!”

He stared down at the torn strips of paper as they drifted to the floor.

"That's it. I'm outta here."

"Wait, Asano," Boo said. "What were you going to say?"

Asano paused. "Oh, yeah. Boo . . . don't trust Kira. She might act like she's your friend . . . but on Planet Kira, if you're her friend instead of mine, she wins. And Kira always has to win."

"That's enough for today, wouldn't you say?" said Quoth, motioning with his wing toward the door.

"Yeah, yeah, I know. I've disappointed everyone AGAIN," Asano said, storming out of the room and slamming the door behind him.

Boo studied until lights out, then got into bed. She lay her head down on the pillow very carefully, afraid some of the knowledge would slosh out.

"Pumpkin?" she whispered. "If Asano's a disappointment . . . what am I?"

"Get some sleep, kiddo," said Pumpkin, already curled at the foot of her bed. "And trust an old cat. You'll do fine."

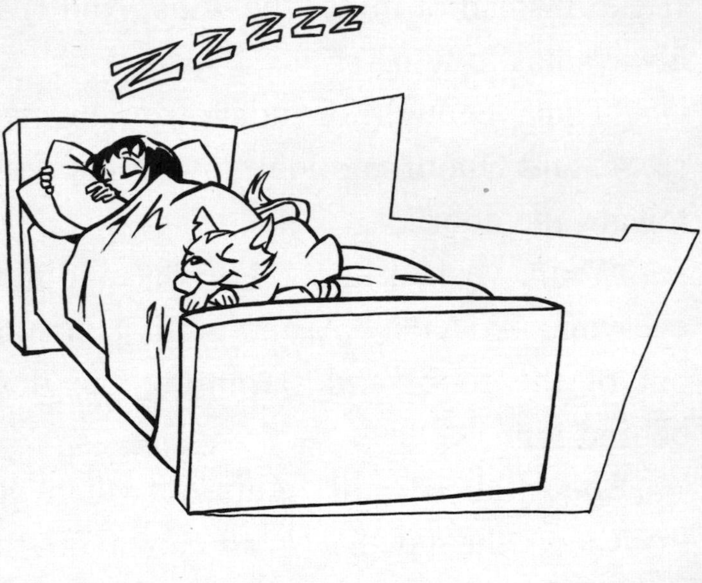

HMPH!
OCH!
AGENT STAR

CHAPTER 4
Test Day

Butterflies were slam-dancing in Boo's stomach on the morning of the Test. She couldn't eat breakfast, even though the cook let the trainees have chocolate cereal.

Then, at eleven hundred hours sharp, the three Agents-to-be and their companion animals were led by Agent Abbot into a room deep in the heart of the Aerie.

There stood three doors, each marked with a letter: A, B, and C.

"Each door leads to a different Test course," Agent Abbot explained. "You will be scored first on how well you complete the puzzles, and second on how fast you finish. Remember: when in doubt, it's more important to be *good* than quick."

"*Some* of us can be both," said Kira, with a toss of her head.

She ran straight for Door A.

Asano turned to Boo and smiled. "Ladies first," he said.

Boo looked at Pumpkin. "Which door should I pick?"

Pumpkin shrugged. "The Test is different each time, so even a veteran like me can't help you."

"Oh well, then. B for Boo, I guess," said the littlest trainee. She took a deep breath and opened Door B.

"See you on the other side!" said Asano, heading for Door C.

STOMP!
+5
BONUS ROUND
zip
+2
+5
ZAP
WHEW! THAT WASN'T SO B--
FIN
+10
+2
Weeeee
+5
CLAMP!
ding!
GUARD ROOM
hold
ZZZZZ ZZZZZ
+5
sneak sneak
SSshh
Tjak!
+5
Tjak!
+10 BONUS!
+2
hold
+5
combination
click! click!
+1
ding!
START
+2
SWOOSH!
+5
+2

"—AAAAD!" Boo clung with all her might to the ledge, and thirty pounds of orange cat clung with all his might to Boo.

"Pumpkin—I can't hold on much longer!" Boo said.

"H E E E E L P !" Pumpkin screamed. "I don't wanna die!"

"And my life hasn't even started yet!" said Boo. "At least you've got *nine* lives!"

"Yeah?" cried Pumpkin. "Well, I've already used *eight* of 'em!"

"HEEEEELP!" They both screamed.

BANG! Came a knock on the wall. And another: BANG! And a third: BANG!

"Kiddo—look!" Pumpkin shouted, tugging on Boo's leg.

"Um, I'm kind of busy!" said Boo, struggling to hold on.

"The cat's right," said Asano, brushing himself off. "Check out this damage! I fought the wall, and I won!"

"But—Asano!" Boo cried. "I can't reach down that far!"

"It's cool," Asano said. "I got the cat's tail." And Pumpkin didn't complain once as Asano pulled Boo and him back to safety.

Kira was waiting when they finally came out of the Test. So was Agent Abbot, and he looked nervous. "I'm sorry I messed up so bad—" Boo started to say.

But Agent Abbot cut her off. "The Aerie is on Orange Alert!" he shouted. "Queen Misery and her Commissars have left Iron City to attack another Parallel World! You're to return to your rooms immediately!"

"But—what about our test results?!" Kira demanded.

"I'm afraid you'll have to wait until tomorrow for those," said Agent Abbot.

"Rats!" Kira grumbled as they walked back to the dorm rooms. "I hate waiting. Hey, Boo—I heard you shouting during the Test. Were you okay?"

"Fine," Boo mumbled.

But no sooner had they gotten back to Room 6 than an alarm began to blare:

"AWOOGA! AWOOGA! CALLING ALL AGENTS!"

"What's that?!" Boo shouted, covering her ears.

"They've figured out where Queen Misery is attacking!" yelled Pumpkin, dashing out the door. "To the Launch Room, kiddo! Ready, set, GO! Last one there's got B.O.!"

"Our first real mission!" squealed Kira, scooping Seeker up and racing after Pumpkin.

"Come on, kiddo!" echoed Pumpkin's voice from down the hall, almost drowned out by the alarm and the sounds of running feet as every Agent in the Aerie sprinted to the Launch Room. "Everyone, get your coats! It's freezing in Snow City!"

Boo lost sight of Pumpkin in the sea of legs. Before she knew it, she had reached the Launch Room.

CHAPTER 5
Calling ~~All~~ most Agents
AGENTS KIRA AND ASANO: LAUNCH!

“That’s everyone, Greycoat,” said Agent Abbot to his companion, a mouse. He turned to step through the gate himself.

“But Agent Abbot, sir—what about me?” Boo asked.

“Not you, Boo,” said Agent Abbot. “I’m sorry. Just . . . behave yourself until we get back.”

“Oh. Yes, sir,” said Boo, her shoulders slumping.

Pumpkin bristled. “Now wait just one cotton-pickin’ minute, Abbot! I got business to settle with Queen Misery!”

“Another day, Pumpkin,” said Agent Abbot as he stepped through. The Gate fizzled out, the alarm shut off, and the Aerie stood in complete silence.

Well, almost. “Come on, kiddo,” said Pumpkin. “When the going gets tough, the tough get ice cream.”

Boo just sighed.

I'VE BEEN TRYING SO HARD, PUMPKIN, BUT IT'S NO USE.
MAYBE I SHOULD JUST GO BACK TO FOURTH GRADE, AND LEAVE SAVING THE MULTIVERSE TO THE GROWN-UPS.
NONSENSE, KIDDO. HEY, YOU WANNA KNOW A SECRET?
AGENT ABBOT? HE STILL SUCKS HIS THUMB.
HEE HEE! REALLY?
Fzzt!
FZZT

THEY FELL FOR IT, MISERY. THE FALSE SIGNALS FROM SNOW CITY.

WELL DONE, NOIR... SEE TO IT THEY NEVER RETURN.

One scoop of Boo-nana,
one scoop of Catnip & Cream

CHAPTER 6
Misery Hates Company

Boo and Pumpkin had just started eating their ice cream when they heard voices and footsteps coming down the hallway.

"Is everyone home already?" Boo asked, jumping up. "Let's go see what they brought back!"

Pumpkin raced after her. "Boo, wait! It's too soon! Something's not right." The hair on his neck bristled. "Besides, that voice . . ."

Boo was already out the door. She couldn't wait to see her friends and hear about their first real mission.

But her smile vanished when she saw who was in the hallway.

It wasn't Kira and Asano.

"Once we change the Gate's frequency, the Agents will be stranded in Snow City forever," said a tall man in a sinister black mask.

Boo didn't recognize the man right away, but she did recognize the woman next to him. A camera for an eye, wires for her hair, and a face as sour as old milk: Queen Misery!

Behind Misery were her henchmen, the Commissars. Their faces were covered in giant masks—except for the one who had spoken—his mask was smaller.

Now Boo knew who he was, from the *Big Book of Space Villains*—Commissar Noir, Misery's most trusted General.

Then Queen Misery saw Boo and screeched like a boiling teakettle. "AAAH! A child!" Misery turned to her favorite Commissar. "Noir! You said there wouldn't be any Agents left!"

"Please don't hurt me!" Boo squeaked.

". . . Hurt you?" said Queen Misery, suddenly honey-sweet. "No, no! I just want to look at you. Come closer, my dear."

"Just want to *look* at her, witch-face?" came Pumpkin's voice. "Yeah, right! And monkeys might fly out of my butt!"

At this, the wires in Misery's hair crackled with electric rage. She turned to the Commissars. "GET THEM!"

“Quick, kiddo!” hissed Pumpkin, swinging his tail as if he were Barry Bonds. “Pitch me one o’ them ice creams.”

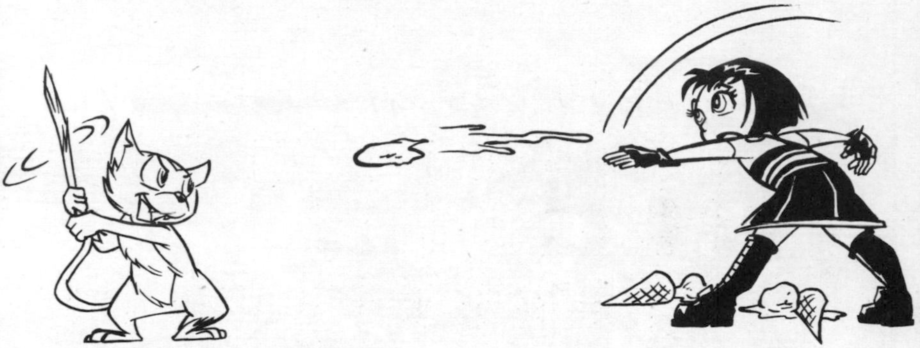

SPLAT! A scoop of Space City’s finest Catnip & Cream hit the lead Commissar in the face. SPLUK! The second Commissar got Boo-nana.

But then Boo was out of ice cream! “What now?” she asked Pumpkin.

“Plan Z,” said Pumpkin.

“What’s Plan Z?” asked Boo.

“The one where we run away, REALLY FAST!”

SOMETIMES IT'S GOOD
TO BE THE LITTLEST

Boo thought about running back to her room and hiding under the bed. Then she decided that would be the first place Queen Misery would look.

But a room that said KEEP OUT—Misery might not look there!

"Do you think we can hide in here, Pumpkin?" whispered Boo.

"Pumpkin?!" she asked again, looking around frantically. And then Boo's spine turned to ice as she realized: Pumpkin was gone!

"Pumpkin. You're slowing down in your old age," Commissar Noir chuckled.

"Hey, have we met?" spat Pumpkin. "Because I think I would have remembered someone with fashion sense as bad as yours."

Pumpkin slashed his claws across Noir's cheek, but Noir just laughed. "Foolish animal. After what I've been through, do you think a cat scratch bothers me?"

GIVE THE CAT TO ME, NOIR. I WANT TO FINISH HIM.
THAT WON'T BE NECESSARY, MY QUEEN. LET'S JUST TIE HIM UP AND GET ON WITH OUR--
THE CAT INSULTED ME! HE MUST DIE!
BUT, OUR OBJECTIVE--
OBEY ME, NOIR!

CHAPTER 7:
Mission: Improbable

Boo sat in the Artifact Room, feeling worse and worse for running away. After all, Pumpkin was the first person—well, cat—who had made her feel like something other than the littlest, most picked-on girl in the fourth grade.

So she decided to search the Artifact Room for something she could use to help. She looked around, but couldn't figure out why it said KEEP OUT on the door. There was nothing in the room but broken toys and dusty junk.

"What use is all this old stuff?" Boo wondered aloud.

MIGHT I SUGGEST THE EGG-TIMER OF IMPROBABILITY?
AAHH!

"That's it over there," said the woman in the mirror, pointing. "Right above The Sneakers of Unspeakable Odor."

"Who are you?" Boo asked.

"I can only answer three questions," said the woman. "Given that there's an evil megalomaniac on the other side of that door, wouldn't you like to ask something a bit more useful?"

"Erm . . . good point," said Boo, reaching for the Egg-Timer. It looked just like the one her mother used in the kitchen, only a lot bigger.

"What does it do?" asked Boo.

"You wind it up and it grants wishes," the woman said brightly. "But only really stupid, improbable ones."

"Oh," said Boo. "But . . . what use is something stupid and improbable?"

"La la la, didn't hear that. What's your last question?" asked the woman in the mirror.

"Sorry. I guess I'm not very good at this," Boo admitted.

"It's okay," said the woman. "You're actually doing pretty well, considering this is your first time talking to a Mirror of Futureflection."

"What's a Mirror of Futu—no, wait a minute," said Boo, stopping herself. "What *should* I wish for, to defeat Queen Misery?"

"Well, she might look tough, but she's really afraid of—" the mirror started to say.

But then—BANG!

RTIFACTS
KEEP
I *THOUGHT* I HEARD VOICES!

Right behind Misery was Noir, still clutching a struggling Pumpkin. "Boo—RUN!" Pumpkin yelled.

Running was exactly what Boo wanted to do, more than anything. But instead she looked Misery right in the eye.

"I have an Egg-Timer, and I'm not afraid to use it!" she shouted. "Release Pumpkin, or . . . else!"

"Or else what?" Misery laughed. "You'll cook breakfast?"

"No," said Boo. She wound the Egg-Timer and whispered, "I wish Queen Misery would fall into a big pit!"

Misery tapped her foot. "Is something going to happen? Because if not, I have an Engineering Room to sabotage."

"Let me check," said Boo. She looked at the Egg-Timer.

It read: INVALID SETTING.

"Oops," mumbled Boo.

Misery snapped her fingers. "Send them through the gate to one of the Shadow Cities! Bone City—no—Ghost Town!"

"Can't we at least rough ′em up a bit?" pleaded a Commissar.

"No," Misery smirked. "Noir is having a sentimental moment. But don't worry—we'll break him of that."

As the Commissars grabbed her, Boo squeezed her eyes shut.

"Monkeys!" she shouted frantically. "Giant space pirate monkeys! In kilts! Flying out of Pumpkin's—"

"DON'T finish that thought!" cried Pumpkin, tucking his tail between his legs.

Boo opened one eye. Nothing.

She opened the other eye.

Still nothing.

"Ha!" cried Misery. "I hate to break it to you, but that toy of yours is bro—"

"Ding!" went the Egg-Timer.

EEW! MONKEYS! I HATE MONKEYS!
YOU HATE EVERYTHING, MY QUEEN.
That's not true. I like broccoli.
STILL, I THINK A TACTICAL RETREAT MIGHT BE IN ORDER.

AVAST, ME HEARTY! I BE SILVERBACK, KING OF THE MONKEY PIRATES.
Whee!
AAH!
No!
Mommy!
Oush!
YEAH, BABY! THAT'S MY GIRL BOO, ROCKIN' THE IMPROBABLE!
Zing!
Swish!

CLUNK!
Swoosh!
Snap!
Arr!
WELL MET, LITTLE AGENT.
Swoop

HURRY UP!
SHOUTING AT ME DOESN'T MAKE ME WORK FASTER.
IT ONLY MAKES ME MAD.
THERE. DONE.
Sha-zam!
COME ON!
?!

WE HAVE TO GET BACK TO IRON CITY!
hm!
Grrr!
NO.
OH, NO!
YOU CREEPS AREN'T GOING ANYWHERE.
Fzzt!

CHAPTER 8
The Agents Come In
from the Cold

"What a waste of time," said Agent Kira, teeth chattering from the cold. "We checked every inch of Snow City, and not a single Commissar!"

"That's the life of an Agent," the Supreme Agent said matter-of-factly. "Not every mission is exciting."

"Thank heavens for that!" said Seeker, teeth chattering from fear *and* the cold.

Quoth puffed out his chest feathers and began to recite:

"Time for us to beat our paths,
To rooms, dry clothes
And nice, hot baths!"

"I'm *so* down with that!" Asano laughed, flicking snow off Quoth's wing.

"For once, something you and I can agree on," grinned Kira. But then, her face turned serious. "I should probably check on Boo. I hope she's not too upset that she had to stay behind."

"Yeah, that was a major bummer," said Asano as they walked down the hall toward their rooms. "I'm actually kinda surprised she wasn't waiting at the gate to welcome us back—"

Then Asano saw something strange, black and broken on the ground. "Hey . . . what's this?"

"Uh-oh," gulped Kira. "That looks awfully sharp. If Boo's done something she shouldn't have—"

ARR!
BE YE HAVIN'
A SIX OF
CLUBS?
MONDAY

AAAAH!
THERE'S A MONKEY IN MY DRAWERS!
OH--HI, KIRA!
GO FISH!

When they heard Kira's scream, the other Agents came running. Soon half the Aerie was peering through the doorway and laughing.

Kira snatched her underwear back from the monkey on her bureau. "Gimme those!" she hissed.

Seeker, with a paw on Kira's leg, gaped at the chaos. "Jings!" he cried.

But Asano's grin was as big as Space City. "I like your style!" he said, high-fiving Boo. "We leave you alone for an hour, and you unleash mad monkey chaos!"

"Well, um . . ." Boo blushed.

"Hey, guys. I wanna see!" yelled an Agent in the back.

Then Agent Abbot's voice rang out above them all. "Make way for the Supreme Agent!" he cried.

And up the Supreme Agent strode. "Would you care to explain what happened while we were gone, Agent Boo?" she asked.

"My Boo kicked butt, that's what happened!" shouted Pumpkin. "By the way, I win," he added, laying down his cards.

"Well, I'll be keel-hauled," swore Silverback. "That be three games in a row!"

"The cat cheats!" cried one of the tied-up Commissars.

"You! Shut it," said Pumpkin to the Commissar. "Unless you want more of the *monkey tickle torture . . .*"

The Commissar gulped. "Sorry . . ." Pumpkin gave him a look of warning. "Pumpkin, Sir!" he added hastily.

"I'm still waiting for an explanation, Boo," repeated the Supreme Agent.

"Well, Pumpkin and I were having some ice cream . . ." And Boo began to tell the story of Queen Misery's attack on the Aerie.

But Boo didn't tell everything. She was worried that she'd get in trouble for going into the Artifact Room.

"I see . . . " said the Supreme Agent. "So how EXACTLY did space pirate monkeys in kilts arrive to save the day?"

Boo stared at her (now not-quite-so-new) boots and said nothing.

"Boo . . . you just saved us from being marooned in Snow City forever," said Agent Abbot. "Whatever you did, you won't be punished. I promise."

Reluctantly, Boo pulled something out from under her pillow and showed it to the Supreme Agent.

"I used the Egg-Timer of Improbability," she said sheepishly. "I'm sorry. I know I wasn't supposed to—"

The Supreme Agent put her hand on Boo's shoulder and smiled. "The things in the Artifact Room shouldn't be used as toys. But you chose wisely. I salute you, Boo.

"And you too, Silverback," she added, with a respectful nod to the monkey King. "Tell your father I'll pop by the Monkeyverse soon, to, ah, renew my acquaintance . . . "

"Aye-aye, Commander," said Silverback with a grin.

Boo blinked. "You're not mad?"

"Not at all," said the Supreme Agent. "Although . . . perhaps it's time for our *guests* to head home." She looked pointedly at the mess in the room.

ARRR, CAP'N! WE BE CATCHIN' YOUR DRIFT AND CASTIN' OFF FOR MONKEY CITY!
YOU BE WELCOME TO VISIT US ANYTIME, AGENT BOO!
BUT. . . I'M NOT A REAL AGENT. I FAILED MY TEST.
SUNDAY

The Supreme Agent motioned for Agent Abbot to come speak with her. They whispered for a few moments.

Then Agent Abbot turned to Boo.

"Boo . . . under the circumstances, we think you've more than earned the right to join us on active duty as a full-fledged Agent . . . with all the rights and privileges thereto."

"Really?" asked Boo. She hardly dared to believe it.

"Really," smiled the Agent Leader.

Boo's heart glowed as if it were full of sunbeams.

Pumpkin strutted over to Boo and gave her a playful swat with his paw. "Didn't I say you'd do just as well as them, kiddo?" said Pumpkin. "You should trust the cat. The cat KNOWS."

"Big things from the littlest Agent!" said Asano, hugging Boo. "I'm proud of you, shorty!"

Boo could hardly believe that only a month ago she'd been sitting in the school auditorium, watching Asano and the other seniors walk past—seniors who would never have been caught dead talking to a fourth grader.

Then Boo remembered the other senior in the room. She looked up at Kira, who was being unusually quiet, and took her hand.

"Hey . . . next time you have a crazy adventure, invite me along, okay?" Kira said, smiling. "Funny. I was so excited to prove myself in Snow City, but the real mission was back here all al—"

Suddenly, Kira's expression changed. "Asano, step AWAY from my poster!"

"It fell off the wall by itself! Honest!" said Asano, not very convincingly.

"He knocked it off!" cried one of the Commissars. "I saw him do it!"

"We'll take these Commissars away for questioning," said Agent Abbot. "You three Agents rest. It's been a long day."

"Wait! I want to ask something about the Artifact Room!" said Boo. "Who was that beautiful woman in the Mirror of Future—um—whatchamacallit?"

Agent Abbot looked at the Supreme Agent. "Should we tell her?"

The Supreme Agent smiled and shook her head. "Don't worry, Agent Boo," she said. "You'll find out when you get older."

THE LITTLEST AGENT

Thank you for visiting Space City!
Come back and see us in Book 2,
The Star Heist, where Boo goes
on her first official mission!

THAT PIPSQUEAK AGENT DOESN'T KNOW WHAT SHE'S DONE! I'LL BURY HER!
AND HER LITTLE CAT TOO!

FRET NOT, MY QUEEN. OUR PLAN CAN STILL PROCEED.

Kat & Mouse™
Bonus Lab Experiment
1 teacher torture
Story: Alex de Campi
Art: Federica Manfredi
When Kat moves to a posh private school, things seem perfect--that is, until a clique of rich, popular kids frame Kat's science teacher dad for stealing school property. Can Kat and her new friend, rebellious computer nerd Mouse, prove who the real culprits are before Kat's dad loses his job?
SPECIAL LOW MANGA PRICE: $5.99
Y
YOUTH AGE 10+
© Alex de Campi and TOKYOPOP Inc.

TOKYOPOP®
A NEW
MANGA CHAPTERS SERIES
from Annie Auerbach, New York Times
bestselling author of Bob's Egg Hunt!
THE GROSSE ADVENTURES™
THE GOOD, THE BAD & THE GASSY™
Brothers Stinky and Stan embark
on the most extraordinary—
albeit smelly—adventures!
TOKYOPOP
THE GOOD, THE BAD & THE GASSY
THE GROSSE ADVENTURES
1
ANNIE AUERBACH
mangachapters
PERFECT FOR
8-10 year olds!
ENJOYABLE
for everyone!
© Annie Auerbach and TOKYOPOP Inc.
mangachapters™